AUTUMN
PUBLISHING

Published in 2020
by Autumn Publishing
Cottage Farm
Sywell
NN6 0BJ
www.igloobooks.com

Autumn is an imprint of Bonnier Books UK

© 2020 MARVEL

0520 001
2 4 6 8 10 9 7 5 3 1
ISBN 978-1-83903-046-8

Printed and manufactured in China

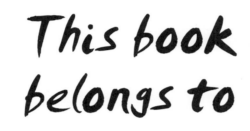

This book
belongs to

....

....

Contents

The New Spider-Man in Town

Miles Morales was a student at Midtown High School in New York City. He was happy and had a thirst for knowledge – especially science. He was a young boy just like any other, working hard and doing the right thing, but something soon happened that changed his life for good...

While in chemistry class, Miles noticed that his good friend – Peter Parker – kept sneaking out of school. Miles grew suspicious, wondering if something was wrong with Peter.

So one day, Miles followed Peter and watched as he snuck a mask from his bag. But it wasn't just any mask that Peter was sneaking – it was Spider-Man's mask!

Miles couldn't believe it. When Peter was leaving school that afternoon, Miles called to Peter, "Hey, Peter, where are you headed?"

Peter awkwardly smiled back and said, "Uh, I've got an assignment for the Daily Bugle... uh... yeah... I've... I've got to go!"

Miles followed Peter to a lab, but lost track of him. Miles didn't notice a genetically altered spider slowly spinning a web and dropping down towards him.

"YEE-OW!" The Spider bit Miles right on the hand! Miles knocked it off. He knew instantly that this was no ordinary spider bite.

Instead of getting ill from the bite, Miles soon discovered that it gave him spider-powers. "I've got to figure out what this means! What should I do?"

He ran home fast.

"Think! Think! Think," Miles told himself. "If Peter really is Spider-Man, then what did he do?" Miles searched for articles about the webbed wonder. "Okay, so you get powers. Check. Then what? You make a costume and go stop bad guys. That seems obvious!"

With that, Miles created his own Spider-Man costume and leapt into the city.

"I can run on walls!" Miles yelled as he scaled the side of a building! He was enjoying discovering his powers, and climbing walls wasn't the only one! Miles soon discovered he had an amazing spider-sense that warned him of danger.

"What the heck?" Miles couldn't ignore the ringing in his brain. That's when he noticed the burglars running behind him. In that instant, what started off as fun became very scary.

Miles had a really big decision to make. Should he run from the danger and stay safe, or should he use his new powers to try to stop the villains?

Miles realised that if he was going to call himself Spider-Man, he was going to have to act like Spider-Man, too!

Much to his surprise, Peter Parker, as the original Spider-Man, was already on the case! One of the criminals was getting away, but Miles joined in. "Hold on helmet head," he announced. "The only place you're racing off to is prison!"

Miles had powers to match Peter's and was easily able to contain the thief.

It wasn't until the action was over that Miles realised just how much danger he was really in. He climbed to the top of a building and wanted to fade way – which is exactly what he did. This was a brand new power, one that even Peter didn't have! He camouflaged himself into his surroundings.

Peter swung up to where Miles had been. "Miles, is that you?" Peter called out. "I recognised your voice. Believe it or not, I know what you're thinking. I went through the same thing when I first got my powers."

Miles was stunned. "You did?"

"Sure, I did," Peter said. "My uncle Ben used to tell me that with great power, there must also come great responsibility."

Peter tossed Miles something from his costume. "Here, you can have these extra web-shooters for now," said Peter.

"Whoa! Cool!" Miles said while testing out the web-shooters.

Miles looked up to Peter, figuring out what he should do.

"Maybe I can follow you around for a few days," he said. "You know, see how it goes?"

"I think that's a good idea, but you can't go around calling yourself Spider-Man, Miles. That name's taken."

"Oh, I'm definitely Spider-Man," Miles said, smiling again. The two swung off together to patrol their friendly neighbourhood.

It wasn't long before Peter got them into quite a pickle – surrounded by some of the nastiest villains in New York City! And that's when Miles knew...

The battle roared while Peter kept poking fun at the rampaging villains. Miles was terrified. "How do you keep joking in the middle of a fight?" he asked Peter. "Aren't you scared?"

That's when Rhino grabbed Peter by the neck. Peter couldn't let out another word — funny or otherwise!

Miles turned and let loose his newest and last power — another power that Peter didn't have at all. Miles would later call it his venom strike! It put Rhino down for the count and Peter was safe!

Miles and Peter wrapped the baddies up in a little more than the usual amount of sticky stuff.

Peter said, "Come on, if you're not going to change your name, you've got to learn how to crack jokes – it's part of the job."

Miles scratched his head, thinking while looking down at the webbed-up villains. Then he said, "Looks like you've got yourselves into a sticky situation, uh, evil-doers."

Peter sighed. "Wow. Somebody call the doctor – you have no funny bone."

MARVEL SPIDER-MAN

A Very Strange Night

Spider-Man has been called many things: amazing, spectacular and sensational. But today, no matter how hard Peter Parker tried, he wasn't feeling amazing, spectacular or sensational. Today, Spider-Man was very, very sleepy. For the last week, Peter hadn't slept through the night.

His dreams were troubling, silly and sometimes downright spooky. A week of nightmares makes for one sleepy crime-fighter.

Peter didn't think much of it, until one very long spider-yawn almost allowed Shocker to ruin the Policeman's Ball! Spider-Man groggily swung into action. He webbed Shocker's gauntlets before knocking the vibrating villain to the floor with a well-timed kick.

"Look! Not only is he a menace, but Spider-Man was sleeping on the job!" shouted J. Jonah Jameson from his table, as Spider-Man swung away.

Spidey knew he needed to see a specialist, someone who was truly an expert on dreams and the human mind. And he knew just the doctor to call.

Doctor Strange explained that he knew all about Spider-Man's sleepless nights.

"The Eye of Agamotto has shown me that you've been experiencing nightmares," Strange told Peter. "And now it will show those nightmares to me."

Soon, Doctor Strange was looking at Spider-Man's nightmares. In some, he was back in elementary school and forgot to wear his trousers. In others, the Sinister Six were winning every battle against him. Doctor Strange was not only able to see the future and the past – he could also see right into a man's very soul.

"Your sleep is interrupted by the supernatural, your dreams are being invaded by the most dastardly of nocturnal threats — your mind is plagued by the villainous Nightmare himself!" declared Strange.

With a snap of his fingers, Strange placed Peter into a deep trance. Then, with the help of the Eye of Agamotto, he dived straight into Peter's dreams.

Peter once again found himself in front of his entire class without his trousers on. Though he was embarrassed, he was no longer alone. Doctor Strange stood tall beside him, urging him to see the nightmare for what it truly was.

Peter concentrated and the class vanished. They were replaced by the master of bad dreams, Nightmare, and his trusty steed, Dreamstalker!

"The Sorcerer Supreme commands you to release your hold on this hero!" shouted Strange. But Nightmare simply laughed.

"I take power from dreams, Doctor Strange," Nightmare began, "and with a hero as strong as Spider-Man, I'll finally be great enough to defeat you!"

As Doctor Strange and Nightmare launched into combat, Peter knew he had to help the Sorcerer Supreme. Even in the dream state, Spider-Man had to lend a hand! He realised he knew just how to do it – by using the power of imagination!

Peter thought and thought and thought, as hard as he could. To his amazement, the dream around him began to change! They weren't in Peter's school any more, but on a giant chessboard, and Spider-Man was in control of the pieces!

"It would seem Spider-Man is using the powers of his own dreams against you!" Doctor Strange said to Nightmare.

Spidey played move after move, defeating Nightmare's pieces, until the villain was the only one left in play.

Outnumbered, the villain retreated, leaving Peter's mind.

"You've won today, Strange, but you've not seen the last of me!" shouted Nightmare, as he rode Dreamstalker out of Peter's mind and back to his home in the shadow realm.

"Don't worry, I look forward to defeating you again," Doctor Strange replied.

Peter woke with a start, pleased to find the good Doctor waiting with a hot cup of tea. "This is Wong's special herbal blend," Doctor Strange said. "It should calm your mind after a night like this."

After saying goodbye to his old friend, the tired hero swung home, changed into his pyjamas and slipped under the sheets. There were no monsters under the bed, and the only things in his wardrobe were his clothes and his spider-suits.

So, for the first time in what felt like weeks, Peter Parker finally got an amazing night's sleep.

The Hunt for Black Panther

Kraven the Hunter loved to hunt wild animals. The only thing he loved more than hunting was the fame that came along with it. But one day, after Kraven had captured a pair of cheetahs, he didn't feel the same sense of accomplishment he normally felt after a successful hunt.

Kraven hungered for a new prey that would give him a real challenge.

But where could he find such a foe?

A few days later, Peter Parker was sent by the Daily Bugle to photograph the annual Protection of Endangered Animals conference in Upper Manhattan. Giving the keynote speech was none other than T'Challa, ruler of the African nation of Wakanda.

Peter was excited for the chance to actually see T'Challa speak.

The king was a compassionate ruler and a scientific genius.

But T'Challa had a secret. He was also the Super Hero Black Panther!

"In order to protect the animals of Earth," the king began, "it is our duty to fight back against illegal hunters and poachers."

Black Panther protected his nation and its animal kingdom from villains by using his superhuman strength, speed and agility. One of those villains was Kraven the Hunter.

Desperate for a new challenge, Kraven knew that this conference was the perfect place to find his next prey – *Black Panther!* The villain burst through the window in a spray of broken glass.

"T'Challa!" he bellowed. "I request a meeting with the Black Panther."

T'Challa's eyes narrowed. "Black Panther will never bow to the likes of you!"

Kraven smirked. "I assumed there would be some protest..."

"… Which is why I brought some backup!" Kraven shouted. Just then, Kraven let out a high-pitched whistle and two cheetahs leapt down from the window above! "No one here is allowed to leave until the Black Panther is mine!"

In the chaos, Peter Parker's spider-senses were tingling like crazy. He knew he had to act fast. This place was turning into a zoo!

Meanwhile, T'Challa's bodyguards, the Dora Milaje, attempted to move the Wakandan king to safety.

"Save your energy," he commanded. "It's time for Black Panther to strike."

Black Panther turned round to discover he had been

joined by Spider-Man!

"What are you doing here?" Black Panther asked.

"Nice to see you, too," said Spider-Man, as he fired a ball of

web fluid at the nearest cheetah. "Stand back – I've beaten

Kraven before. I can deal with these overgrown house cats."

"Spider-Man, no! You must be careful!" Black Panther tried to

warn the web-slinger, but it was already too late.

"Whoa! Nice kitty!" Spider-Man exclaimed as the cheetah grabbed his web and lunged towards him.

Acting fast, Black Panther grabbed the cheetah before Spider-Man was harmed.

"Listen to me. My animal instincts tell me that these creatures are being held here against their will. They will only attack you if they are provoked."

But Spidey wasn't out of danger yet! Kraven threw a spear at the web-slinger, who rolled out of the way just in time!

"I'll calm them down while you get Kraven," Black Panther said to Spidey.

"On it!" Spider-Man said as he swung towards the balcony.

Black Panther massaged the backs of the cheetahs' heads, safely pressing down on their pressure points to relax the animals' anger.

"That should calm you down," he said, petting the cheetahs.

With the cheetahs under control, Spider-Man caught up with the villainous hunter, who began throwing knives at the web-slinging hero. Unfortunately for Kraven, Spidey's trusty spider-sense made it impossible for him to land an attack.

"What's the matter, Kraven?" Spider-Man asked. "Can't catch a little spider?"

"Maybe it would help if you took care of that smell first, Kraven. Yuck! Do they not have showers in the jungle?" Spider-Man joked.

Blinded with anger, Kraven was unable to focus on the fight with the two Super Heroes. Spider-Man quickly used his web-shooters to disarm Kraven, giving Black Panther the perfect opening for an attack.

"Now you will pay for the crimes you have committed against the animal kingdom!" Black Panther added, before delivering the final blow to Kraven. The hunter was clearly no match for the strength and speed of the King of Wakanda.

Kraven was finally defeated.

"Beaten by a spider and a cat," Kraven mumbled.

"What's wrong? Don't like being held in captivity?" Spider-Man asked.

Black Panther addressed the crowd of frightened spectators. "You are all safe! These majestic creatures are not the enemy. They deserve respect and compassion. And thank you, Spider-Man, for helping me save them."

Spider-Man was caught off guard by the Black Panther's kind words. "Wow. Thanks, Black Panther. Now might not be a good time, but do you mind if we take a selfie?"

The Widow's Sting

Spider-Man was casually swinging through the streets of New York City. It was the weekend, and crime-fighting had been kind of quiet, not that he was complaining. Sometimes a Super Hero could use a nice day of just wall-crawling and web-slinging.

Looking down, he thought he saw a familiar face in the shadows. He swung over to take a closer look.

Landing on top of a building, he found himself face-to-face with the famous Avenger, Black Widow! "Hey, Widow! Making the rounds?" Spidey asked.

At first, Black Widow looked surprised to see him, but then she smiled.

Spider-Man noticed she was staring at something. He followed her gaze to Avengers Tower in the distance. "If you're looking to head home soon, I could give you a ride," he offered. "Spidey-style."

Black Widow's smile grew. "Yes, it would be wonderful to see the Avengers again."

Again? Spidey thought. ***Black Widow is an Avenger. Wouldn't she be there all the time?*** But Spider-Man, not being an Avenger himself, shrugged it off.

Black Widow climbed onto Spider-Man's back. "Hold on," he said, as they swung towards Avengers Tower.

When they arrived at the tower, Spider-Man walked up to the security door and placed his hand on the scanner.

"Avengers Guest, Spider-Man. Identity: Confirmed. Welcome," the computerized voice said.

"What a friendly building," Spidey noted.

The doors opened and Spider-Man began to walk inside.

Black Widow started to follow, but Spider-Man stopped her. "Don't you have to check in?"

Black Widow lifted her cold eyes. Spider-Man's spider-sense tingled.

"Of course," said Black Widow, reluctantly placing her hand on the security scanner.

The alarm began to sound. "Identity unknown. Intruder alert! Intruder alert!"

Black Widow, or whoever this imposter was, suddenly raised her arm and destroyed the scanner with her wrist blaster.

"Hey! That was a very friendly computer. You didn't have to blow it up like that, *Fake* Widow," Spider-Man said.

The Black Widow imposter lunged at Spider-Man.

She was trying to get into Avengers Tower!

Spider-Man fired a web towards her, but the imposter vaulted through the air and landed gracefully on her feet behind him.

"Thanks for the ride," she said. "You even held the door for me. Such a gentleman." Black Widow ran towards the open door – only to have it slam in her face!

"I guess you're not on the guest list," Spider-Man said.

Frustrated, the false Black Widow blasted the doors, but they still didn't budge. "I don't think they're going to let you in," said Spider-Man.

As Spider-Man and the imposter began to fight, a familiar-looking shield blocked one of the blasts that was about to hit Spider-Man. Another bolt of energy came shooting down from above, landing near the imposter's feet.

Looking up, Spider-Man saw two of his Avenger friends coming to his aid: Captain America and Iron Man!

With their help, Spider-Man continued to fight with the false Black Widow.

She flipped and dodged Cap's shield as she fired her wrist blaster at Iron Man. "If only you had stepped aside and let me through, Spider-Fool."

"Sorry, rules are rules. I don't want to lose my guest pass," Spidey quipped, dodging one of the phony Widow's blasts.

Iron Man dived down, but the imposter was too fast, flipping over him and grabbing on to his back.

"You shouldn't give rides to strangers, Iron Man," the villain said.

Suddenly, Captain America's shield flew from behind and struck the imposter in the knees, knocking her to the ground with a thud.

Swinging into action, Spider-Man quickly webbed the evildoer's hands together, jamming the wrist blasters.

"I think it's time we find out who is behind the Black Widow mask," Spidey said.

Spider-Man pulled on the imposter's hair, but instead of a wig coming off in his hands, the foe's entire body changed! Where Black Widow had been, there now lay the pale-faced villain... the Chameleon!

The Chameleon was a master of disguise, and his suit gave him the ability to take on the form of anyone.

"I thought Black Widow was looking a little pale today," Spidey said.

"And you nearly fell for it, too," the Chameleon snarled.

As Iron Man flew away with the Chameleon, Spider-Man turned to Captain America. "I hope this doesn't mean I'm banned from Avengers Tower for life."

Cap laughed. "Spider-Man, if you hadn't made sure that imposter followed the rules, the Chameleon would have been able to sneak in. You're always welcome here, son."

Spidey was relieved. "Good, can we go inside now? Avengers Tower has the best video games and snacks in town."

MARVEL
SPIDER-MAN
Mega Meltdown

New York City was in the middle of a heat wave. Unfortunately for Spider-Man, that wasn't going to stop the city's criminals.

"Seriously, guys? Committing crimes in a city full of Super Heroes? Not a great idea," Spider-Man said to the two bank robbers he had just webbed.

Despite the heat, Spider-Man noticed that the criminals were shivering.

"If we're going to be stuck here, how about some more webbing, huh?"

Why were those guys acting like it's cold? Spider-Man thought as he swung away. *It's been a scorcher for weeks!*

As he swung closer to Times Square, Spider-Man's spider-sense began to tingle. The wind started to whip around him as the temperature steadily dropped.

Maybe it is a little chilly today.

Just then, Spider-Man came across the source of the changing weather. A gigantic portal had opened up in the sky, sending snow flurries down upon the city.

Loki, the trickster god of Asgard, was standing on a skyscraper clutching a Cosmic Cube!

Spider-Man swung down to confront the Super Villain.

"Ah, the Spider. I invite you to witness the start of my glorious reign," Loki said proudly.

"Yeah, right," Spider-Man said. "What are a few snowflakes going to do?"

"Just wait until you meet my friends," Loki cackled.

Suddenly, a group of Frost Giants leapt from the portal! Parked cars were crushed under the weight of the massive giants as they lumbered through the streets. Frightened tourists ran for cover as sparks from collapsing billboards rained down upon them. "Meet the Frost Giants of Jotunheim," Loki said in an otherworldly voice. "Now that I have the Cosmic Cube, they are under my control!"

Spider-Man knew there was only one thing to do.

He leapt into action.

Thwip! Spidey shot his webs through the air. He sailed over Times Square, straight towards one of the giants.

"Hey, Snowball! Over here!" Spider-Man shouted.

As he got closer to the giants, he narrowly missed a massive club swinging towards him.

"What do I look like — some kind of bug?" he said. Spider-Man looked down at his suit. "Oh, yeah, well, I can't really blame you."

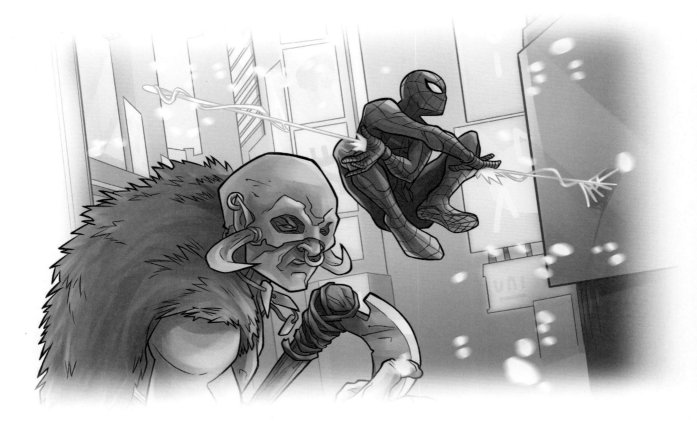

Spider-Man swung out of reach, then approached the Frost Giants once more. The mindless giants paid him no attention. They were only concerned with one thing: destruction.

I don't have enough webbing left to tie up Frosty and friends, Spidey thought. *But this should slow them down.*

Spider-Man fired a web across the street. He hoped this barrier would stop the Frost Giants' march.

It looked like the Frost Giants were finally going to be stopped when... BOOM! Spider-Man was shocked to witness the Frost Giants step on his web barrier, causing two billboards to crash to the ground.

Just then, Spider-Man spotted an Avengers Quinjet flying over.

"It's about time!" Spidey exclaimed. He knew that with friends like Captain America, Thor, Black Widow and Iron Man on his side, Loki and his snow buddies didn't stand a chance!

Spider-Man approached the jet as it landed on a nearby rooftop. As the cargo ramp lowered, Spider-Man saw only one hero. One very small hero.

"Ant-Man?!" Spider-Man was shocked as the miniature hero walked down the ramp. "Where's everyone else?"

"The Avengers are busy with Thanos," Ant-Man said. "That guy never takes a day off. Nick Fury called and said there was some trouble in the city. I'm here to back you up, pal."

"No offence, but I was expecting some bigger guns," Spider-Man said. "How are two bugs going to stop three giants?"

"Well, looks like these 'two bugs' are all New York has today," replied Ant-Man, as he grabbed on to Spidey's suit and the pair headed back towards the wintry chaos.

As soon as Spider-Man
and Ant-Man rejoined the Frost Giants,
one of them threw a car at the two heroes.

"Look out!" Ant-Man exclaimed.

"Way ahead of you!" Spider-Man responded as he
swiftly dodged the car. "But this heavy snowfall isn't making
anything easier! Any ideas?"

"Well, if they want to head to Central Park, I can send in some
ants to ruin their picnic," Ant-Man said sarcastically.

"Even so, it's not warm enough for a picnic," Spider-Man said. "But wait! That gives me an idea! How much do you know about electricity?"

"More than you, kid," Ant-Man said. "And I think I know where you're going with this."

Evading attacks from Loki's Frost Giants, Spidey swung towards Times Tower, the brightest building in the city.

As Spider-Man approached the tower, Ant-Man was able to jump just before a Frost Giant grabbed Spider-Man's webbing. The giant pulled the webs, yanking him off of the tower.

"Oomph!" Spider-Man exclaimed as he crashed onto the hard cement.

Ant-Man knew Spider-Man couldn't hold back the giants for long. He squeezed between the bright billboards. Once inside, the small hero was able to hack into the main power grid.

"Hey, you big bullies!" Ant-Man shouted. "How about turning up the heat!"

Suddenly, Times Square began to brighten. The lights became brighter and brighter until the light from the billboards was blinding. Hit with 161 megawatts of power, the Frost Giants quickly began to shrink until they vanished completely.

"It's working!" Spider-Man said as he swung to face Loki. "Looks like your Frost Giants should've brought some sun cream."

"Spider-Man!" Loki roared. "You did this?"

Spider-Man quickly shot a web straight towards Loki. "I had some help. Not too bad for a couple of bugs, huh?"

With Loki blinded by webbing, Spider-Man was able to take the Cosmic Cube out of his grasp. Using the power of the Cosmic Cube, Spider-Man opened up a portal and sent Loki back to Jotunheim.

"I'll be back, Spider – I always come back!" Loki screamed as he was pulled into the portal at high speed.

"Defeated Loki, melted a bunch of Frost Giants and caused a blackout in Times Square," Ant-Man said. "Man, we deserve a holiday."

"You're right," Spider-Man responded. "But we still have to return this cube and restore power to Times Square."

"Yeah, but first... Spider! My ants and I challenge thee to a snowball fight!" Ant-Man said, mocking Loki.

"You're on!" replied Spider-Man.

Spider-Men

Young Miles Morales and his friend Ganke were on a school trip when they were caught by surprise. "Ganke, watch out!" Miles shouted to his best friend.

A flood of wild animals came stampeding towards them right in the heart of the Central Park Zoo!

Miles knew he had to help, but he couldn't put on his spider-suit. Ganke was the only one who knew about his powers. Putting on his suit would reveal Miles's secret identity!

"How did all these animals escape?" Ganke asked.

As if the universe was answering his question, Rhino charged out of the woods and came barrelling down on Miles and Ganke. Ganke shouted at Miles, "Jump, dude! He's going to run you over!"

Luckily for Miles, the original Spider-Man snagged Rhino's horn just in time to save Miles from revealing his secret – and from a LOT of bruises.

"Yeehaw! You're worse than a bucking bronco, Rhino!" Spider-Man shouted.

When Miles realised that THE Spider-Man was there to help, he was thrilled.

Rhino jerked his head away, yanking Spidey off his back. WHAM! Spidey slammed down into the ground.

"Ha!" Rhino bellowed. "Try and keep up, Spider-Man. My new animal friends and I are pretty wild."

As Peter lay on his back, Miles rushed over to see if he was okay. "Hey, Pe—uh, I mean, Spider-Man," Miles said.

Peter was still a little woozy from hitting the ground.

"Miles! Great to see you, buddy..." But before Peter could finish, he felt Rhino's hand grab his ankle.

Rhino flung Spidey through the air. As Peter whizzed by, he asked Miles, "How are your grades holding uuuuup?"

Miles stood face-to-face with Rhino, but he didn't budge. Not one inch.

"You've got nerve, kid," Rhino snorted. "You're lucky I got the web-head to finish, otherwise I'd teach you a lesson!"

Rhino stormed off to find Peter Parker. He didn't realise that Miles was also a Spider-Man.

Miles looked left and right. All of his classmates, even Ganke, were gone! He remembered what Peter once told him: "With great power comes great responsibility."

Without a second thought, Miles slipped on his mask and pulled on his suit.

Where Miles once stood, now bounced the one and only (well, one of only two) Spider-Man! Miles's kick to Rhino's head was enough to give Peter a chance to get loose from the Super Villain's grip! "Thanks for the assist, Spider-Man," Peter said.

"How cute, the Spider-Men have come to meet their doom," Rhino snarled.

As Peter dodged Rhino's attacks, he called to Miles, "I need you to wrangle the zoo animals before they cause any more damage!"

Miles was hurt. "You don't want my help battling Rhino?"

Before Peter could respond, Rhino poked his horn right into Peter's behind!

Why does Peter not want my help? Miles thought to himself. **Maybe I'm not cut out for this whole Super Hero thing after all.** But just when Miles began to doubt himself, he remembered there was a job to do. It was his responsibility to wrangle the animals, and if that's what Peter needed, then that's exactly what he was going to do!

With great care, Miles wrestled a crocodile, webbing its mouth so it couldn't bite anyone. Using his wall-crawling ability, Miles climbed a large tree and guided a fluffy red panda to safety.

Then, Miles contained a lion by electrifying the air using his venom strike. Eventually, Miles helped all the animals find their habitats.

As Miles stood in front of the contained animals, he began to wonder where Peter and Rhino were.

"Ow. Ow. OW!" Suddenly Peter came bouncing across the pavement and slammed to a stop next to Miles.

"Rough landing," Peter joked. "Man, where's another Spider-Man when you need him?"

"Seriously, dude?" Miles asked.

Even though Miles was still learning his powers, Peter knew he was ready. "What do you say, Miles — you want to see if Rhino can beat the Spider-Men?"

Miles smiled. "I thought you'd never ask!"

Together, the Spider-Men made the ultimate team.

"Have a nice trip!" Peter said as he webbed up Rhino's feet.

"Man, your ugly mug is shocking!" Miles said as he used his venom strike to give Rhino an unexpected jolt.

"Oooh, nice one!" Peter cheered.

Rhino slammed into the pavement, knocking himself out cold. "Do you want to make the final wisecrack?" Peter asked.

Miles smiled. "How's this? Spider-Men: we put the NO in Rhino."

Peter burst into laughter and let out a theatrical sob. "My little baby is all grown up!"

After taking care of Rhino, the Spider-Men settled down for a well-deserved lunch break. "Remember when I told you that true heroes give back to their community?" Peter asked. Miles nodded as he took a loud sip of his drink.

"Well, giving the Central Park Zoo a dude dressed as a rhino wasn't exactly what I had in mind."

Miles grinned. "Still... he definitely fits in."

The Amazing Incredible Spider-Hulk

One day, Spider-Man was with the Hulk when a little girl shyly asked the green giant for his autograph.

The Hulk agreed, but when he tried, the pencil snapped. He told Spider-Man that he wished he was, as he put it, "More puny like Bug-Man."

"Sometimes I'd rather be more like you," replied Spider-Man.

The pair then headed to S.H.I.E.L.D. headquarters to see a new invention.

When they arrived, Nick Fury was standing next to a device that held an enormous purple gemstone. Fury explained that the machine would allow two Super Heroes to temporarily swap abilities.

Spidey and the Hulk were very excited. It would be like switching places! When Fury asked for volunteers, two hands immediately went up.

Project A.S.S.E.M.B.L.E.
Ability Switching and
Super-power Exchange
Mighty Big Laser Engine.

Spider-Man and the Hulk stood side by side over a big red X on the floor. Fury activated the device. The machine started to hum and the purple gemstone glowed. It shot out a beam, covering both the Hulk and Spider-Man.

But the machine overheated, causing an explosion that shook the room! When the smoke cleared, everyone stared at the figure standing on the red X.

It wasn't Spidey. It wasn't the Hulk.

It looked like both of them... combined! Two heroes had merged into one hybrid creature – the Spider-Hulk!

Peering at Iron Man's armour, Spider-Hulk studied his reflection in its gleaming surface. The face that stared back at him was familiar, and yet... unfamiliar.

Confused and frustrated, Spider-Hulk couldn't control his feelings.

"Bug-Hulk SMASH!" he yelled, pounding his fists into the floor. Captain America tried to calm down the hybrid hero, but Spider-Hulk grabbed Cap's shield and flung it into the wall. Then the frightened Spider-Hulk turned and crashed through the glass window. The Avengers raced after him.

Spider-Hulk couldn't think clearly. It felt as though there were two separate voices in his head! He just wanted to get away from the people trying to capture him. He didn't realise his pursuers were his friends, the Avengers.

"Bug-Hulk's bug-sense tingling," he muttered to himself.

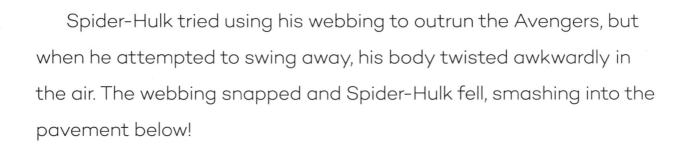

Spider-Hulk tried using his webbing to outrun the Avengers, but when he attempted to swing away, his body twisted awkwardly in the air. The webbing snapped and Spider-Hulk fell, smashing into the pavement below!

With Spider-Hulk momentarily weakened, Hawkeye quickly came up with a plan. He had sometimes calmed the Hulk down with a nursery rhyme, so he sat down and began reading to Spider-Hulk. It worked too well. The hybrid hero thought it was bedtime and he fled looking for a midnight snack!

This gave Black Widow an idea. The Avengers would draw Spider-Hulk back to S.H.I.E.L.D. headquarters using the one thing both Spider-Man and the Hulk loved: food! When Thor and Black Widow found Spider-Hulk, he was ransacking every hot dog cart in the city looking for snacks. Thor stood in his path and tried to lure Spider-Hulk away with a delicious chocolate cake from the bakery.

But before Thor could lead the way back to headquarters, Spider-Hulk swallowed the entire cake. The new Super Hero also had a super appetite!

Iron Man knew that Spider-Man was really Peter Parker, a teenager who couldn't resist his Aunt May's famous wheat cakes. So the armoured Avenger instructed his personal chef to make enough wheat cakes to feed a small country. In other words, enough to feed one Spider-Hulk.

Iron Man zoomed around the city, leaving a trail of wheat cakes for his fused friends to follow. It worked!

The Spider-Hulk gobbled each tasty treat, leading him closer and closer to the device that caused all this chaos in the first place.

Spider-Hulk was so busy wolfing down wheat cakes that he didn't notice he was sitting on the big red X. He swallowed the last piece of wheat cake and said, "Spider-Hulk wants maple—"

But before he could finish his sentence, Nick Fury pressed the reverse button.

Once again the purple gemstone glowed and Spider-Hulk was shot with an energy beam. When the light faded, two heroes stepped forth: Spider-Man and the Hulk!

"I really learnt something today," Spider-Man told the Hulk. "I used to think I wanted to be more like you. But being Spider-Hulk just... didn't feel like me. And I like being me."

The green goliath nodded. "Hulk learnt something, too," he began. "Hulk learnt that Bug-Man's puny costume is bad fit on Hulk-size body!"

The two friends laughed. Then they patted their bellies and turned to the other Avengers.

"Okay," Spider-Man said with a wink, "who's up for some dessert?"

Reptile Rampage

Dr Curtis Connors, also known as the Lizard, was in trouble. Peter Parker knew it as soon as he saw all the pictures of the Lizard splashed across the front page of the Daily Bugle. Peter also knew that his boss, J. Jonah Jameson, would be mad that Peter hadn't delivered exclusive pictures of the Lizard.

As soon as Peter walked into the Daily Bugle, J. Jonah Jameson called him into his office.

"Parker, the Lizard is on the loose, and I need pictures," he demanded. "I don't care if you have to camp out in a swamp. I want a shot for the front page. And I also want a picture of Spider-Man fighting the Lizard," J.J.J. shouted. He always expected perfection.

"I'm your man. I'll get you those shots," Peter told his boss.

Meanwhile, Dr Connors's wife, Martha, was very upset. She'd noticed her husband mixing up a strange formula earlier that week. She knew that he was trying to create a serum that would help him grow back his missing arm, but she also knew that it came with a serious side effect. It turned Dr Connors into an evil villain called the Lizard!

Spider-Man found Martha
Connors sitting on her porch. She was
looking at a picture of her husband.

"I wish he didn't care about growing
back that arm." She looked at Spider-Man with concern.

"I'll find him," Spidey told her. "Don't worry."

"Please hurry," Mrs Connors said. "You need to bring him
to the lab and feed him the antidote."

"Got it! He won't be a lawless lizard much longer. Soon he
will be back to being good old Dr Connors."

Spidey searched New York City
up and down. Finally, he spotted
the Lizard. Spider-Man chased him into
an ice cream shop, hoping to lock the cold-blooded
beast in a freezer, which would diminish the Lizard's strength.
Unfortunately for Peter, the Lizard escaped!

"I'm not a fan of frozen treatsss," the Lizard hissed at Spidey.

"If you try to run from me, you're going to be on a rocky road," Spidey taunted.

The Lizard stomped through the streets, creating a wave of destruction, crushing car windows and damaging shopfronts.

Spidey trailed behind the Lizard as they made their way up the building where Dr Connors kept his lab.

"Once you go in there, I can promise you're not coming out," Spidey said as he scaled the side of the building. The Lizard tried to knock Spidey down with his powerful tail, but it didn't work.

The Lizard roared, and it echoed through the city. People came out from the surrounding buildings and crowded around to see the excitement. Spider-Man was going to save the day!

Spider-Man found a
window to climb through and
made his way into the lab, grabbing the antidote.

Suddenly, the Lizard crashed through the door, followed by a group
of angry reptiles. The Lizard had given them something that let him
completely control their minds. They were ready to attack! Spider-Man
looked to his left and saw a giant snake slithering towards him.

"Yikes!" Spider-Man shouted as the monstrous snake coiled itself around his leg. Spidey quickly fired webs at the Lizard as more and more reptiles attacked.

The Lizard dodged Spider-Man's webs and swung his enormous tail. Spidey flew through the air, crashing straight into the lab table. But Spider-Man kept firing his webs! He didn't know if he was going to be able to fight both the Lizard and the cold-blooded fiends.

Spider-Man was in full battle mode
with the reptiles when the Lizard threw a
desk at him.

"Whoa, bad lizard!" Spidey called out.
"Dr Connors, do you realise what you are
doing? You have to stop the Lizard!"

But it was pointless. Dr Connors had
no control once the Lizard was unleashed.
There was no use reasoning with
a monster.

In between fighting, Spidey eyed the antidote. The Lizard used the opportunity to unleash his final attack. He ordered the reptiles to hold Spidey down as he began to strike him over and over. Spider-Man fought back hard, making sure not to bump into the antidote. Finally, Spidey broke free, grabbed the antidote and poured it into the Lizard's open jaws.

Within seconds, the Lizard began
to morph until he slowly became
Dr Connors again. Spider-Man was
relieved to see the doctor's familiar face.

"Wow, what happened?"
Dr Connors asked.

"It's a long story," Spidey sighed.

Soon Martha Connors had her husband back,
and J. Jonah Jameson had his front-page spread.
Everyone was happy!

That night, Peter came home to one of Aunt May's amazing home-cooked meals.

"How was your day, Peter?" Aunt May asked.

Peter didn't even know where to begin. Aunt May didn't know Peter was Spider-Man, and he certainly couldn't tell her about his fight with the Lizard. "Don't forget to save room for dessert, Peter," Aunt May said as Peter finished his dinner. "I picked up a pint of ice cream. Your favourite, rocky road."

Seeing Spots

It was a wonderfully sunny day. Peter Parker and Gwen Stacy were strolling through Central Park, about to buy hot dogs from a vending cart. "Ketchup, mustard and relish?" Peter asked.

"You know me too well, Parker," Gwen said, smiling.

Peter reached into his pocket to pay for the hot dogs when Gwen reached for her purse. "My treat," she said.

Before Peter could argue, a strange black circle appeared below Gwen's purse. The friends were shocked when a white arm covered in black spots came shooting out of the hole. It grabbed Gwen's purse! Another circle appeared above them. Inside, a man's head appeared.

A menacing voice erupted from the circle. "What a lovely bag. I'm sorry, but I don't believe there will be any hot dogs today."

As suddenly as they appeared, the thief and his black circles disappeared. Gwen was shocked. Peter's eyes narrowed. He was not going to let some freaky villain ruin his perfect day with Gwen.

"Wait here!" Peter exclaimed. Before Gwen could say anything, Peter bolted out of sight.

Peter ducked into an alley and changed into his Spider-Man suit to chase down the thief. He was a robber called the Spot! Swinging high, Spider-Man looked out over the streets of New York for signs of the criminal.

"Ha! I *spot* you!" he chuckled as he saw black circles appear beside another potential victim.

He swung off to face his foe.

Spider-Man managed to web the purse before the Spot could snatch it.

"Spider-Man! I've been waiting to run into you," the Spot said. "Over and over."

Suddenly, black circles appeared all around Spidey. Out of them came fists, hitting Spider-Man as the Spot appeared and reappeared in different directions.

The villain was so fast that even Spider-Man's spider-sense couldn't keep up.

Spider-Man fell, beaten by the Spot. The teleporting villain appeared over him, laughing.

"Better luck next time, Bug-Brain!" the Spot taunted, vanishing into thin air.

Feeling woozy, Spidey realised he was going to need some help defeating this new menace.

Fortunately, he knew just who to call.

Spidey swung to an abandoned church, hoping this was still the place his friends used as a hideout.

"If anyone can help me, it'll be these two," he muttered, knowing he was running out of options. The Spot was going to be hard to defeat.

Although they had only teamed up a few times before, and one of the two could be kind of creepy, Spider-Man knew he could trust this duo to help him get the job done.

"Cloak! Dagger! Man, am I glad to see you guys," Spider-Man said as he entered the church. He quickly filled them in on his encounter with the Spot.

"I need your help." Spidey turned to Cloak. "I know you're used to popping in and out of thin air, too."

"I have felt someone tapping into my teleportation force recently," Cloak noted. "It seems this Spot and I share a connection through multiple dimensions."

That gave Dagger an idea. "If we can follow the energy Cloak is feeling, it could lead us to the Spot. Then my light daggers could help trap him there by draining his energy."

With the plan set, the heroes dived into the darkness of Cloak's cape and disappeared.

When the trio reappeared, they found themselves in the Spot's secret hideout. It was filled with all the stolen purses, jewels and other items the thief had taken on his crime spree.

"Spider-Man! How did you find me here? And who are these freaks?" the Spot asked, shocked.

Spider-Man just smiled. "Looks like you're not the only disappearing act in town, Spot."

The Spot tore the teleporting discs off of his suit, threw them around the room, and started to dive into them. He was ready to attack! But this time, the good guys were ready, too.

Bright knives shot out of Dagger's hands and burst into the dark circles. Her illuminating power filled the darkness in which the Spot thrived.

They pushed out the Spot, cutting off his escape.

Spider-Man quickly webbed the villain before he could try his teleportation tricks again. "Hmm, looks like you're stuck. I guess you could say my webs are *spot-* on!"

Dagger chuckled at Spider-Man's bad joke, while Cloak's icy stare never wavered. Their plan worked!

The Spot's thieving days were over.

The heroes helped return the stolen items. As the pile grew smaller, Spidey recognised one of the purses and grabbed it.

"Not enough pockets in your suit?" Dagger asked with a wink.

"Hey, bad jokes are my thing," Spider-Man replied.

Then with a quiet whoosh, Cloak whisked Dagger and the Spot away.

Back in Central Park, Peter Parker came running back to Gwen. There was a police officer handing over her purse.

"Gwen! You got it back!" Peter exclaimed.

"It was incredible, Peter! Spider-Man caught the thief and brought all the stolen items back – including my purse."

Peter blushed. "Wow, he's a real hero."

"But you are just as brave, Peter," Gwen said, hugging her friend. "Thanks for looking out for me."

Peter grinned. "I'm sorry I couldn't do more."

"Well," Gwen said, handing the hot dog vendor money, "you certainly did enough to earn this hot dog. My treat, as promised."

"You're the best," Peter said as he chewed. "Wow, this really hits the *spot*."

The Attack of the Portal Crashers

BOOM! A tremendous noise echoed through the streets of New York City. The ground shook so hard that car alarms went off and stray cats hid under bins.

Spider-Man looked down, his spider-sense on high alert. He immediately spotted Iron Man fighting a strange feathery villain.

It was Spider-Man's old enemy – the Vulture!

Spider-Man swooped in to help.

Working together, Spider-Man and Iron Man defeated the Vulture in no time.

"Thanks, kid," Iron Man said. "We make a pretty great team."

"You're welcome, Mr Stark," Spider-Man said, blushing under his mask. Iron Man, billionaire Tony Stark, was a big deal.

"Please, Mr Stark was my father," Iron Man joked. He put his arm around Spidey. "You know, some of the greatest victories have been won by heroes working as a team. Like the time Cap, Falcon and I teamed up to fight Hydra, or when A.I.M. were taken down by Widow and Hawkeye."

"Well, I usually work alone," Spider-Man explained. "I don't think I've earned my place among the real heroes yet."

"There's no shame in needing a little help," Iron Man said with a smile. "See ya around, kid." As Iron Man rocketed away, Spider-Man began to think about how cool all the other heroes were, and how badly he wanted to prove himself. That gave him an idea. What if he threw a party for them?

They deserved it – they saved the world every day, after all.

That night, Spider-Man went home and took off his suit.
At home, he could be just regular old Peter Parker. The more Peter
thought about it, the better he liked the idea of throwing a party
for the other heroes. *A great party would definitely impress the
Avengers!* he thought.

Peter immediately got to work. He wrote invitations to all the
Super Heroes he could think of. He knew Central Park would be the
perfect place to host the party. He'd bake a cake and maybe even
make a piñata. It was going to be awesome!

Peter's invitations made their way to every

famous Super Hero in the world.

But one invitation made its way – entirely by

accident – through a rogue wormhole right into the hands

of Thanos, the cosmic Super Villain.

"All of Earth's Mightiest Heroes in one place?" Thanos

said, reading the invitation. "This is my chance to destroy

them all in one blow!"

The party started out great. Peter served delicious cupcakes and even made a Mysterio-shaped piñata. Everyone showed up and brought things for the party! Hulk had baked a green cake. Doctor Strange put on a dazzling light show. Hawkeye set up an indestructible game of whack-a-mole, and laughed as a frustrated Thor whacked away at it with his hammer. Captain America and Black Widow were playing Frisbee with Cap's shield, and Black Panther was beating Ant-Man at the pin-the-staff-on-the-Loki game.

Everyone was having a great time!

Suddenly, the sky turned dark and stormy. Lightning cracked against the grey clouds.

"We're under attack!" Captain America shouted as thousands of alien cyborgs started raining down on Central Park.

"It's the Chitauri!" Black Widow yelled.

Every hero leapt into action.

The scene fell into chaos as the world's greatest heroes battled the galaxy's fiercest enemy. With a zap of her electrostatic cuffs, Black Widow took out several cyborgs, while Thor plowed through another dozen with his hammer. Iron Man and Captain America blasted Chitauri to pieces. Black Panther slashed at them with his vibranium claws. And as for Hulk... well, Hulk SMASHED!

Spider-Man watched in awe. Every hero was needed in this fight — and that included him! He threw himself into the battle, firing webs at lightning speed.

The greatest Super Heroes in the world, including Spider-Man, fought long and hard. Soon the tide of the battle was turning. Fallen cyborgs littered the ground.

But then, with a mighty CRACK, the sky split open and Thanos appeared. Spider-Man's heart sank. The Chitauri were bad news, but Thanos was way worse. The world was really in trouble now.

"I've got him!" cried Captain America. But Thanos saw Cap charging and threw him into a tree. Then Black Panther leapt at Thanos, kicking powerfully, but the blow bounced right off Thanos's chest. Doctor Strange's magic couldn't contain the massive villain, and even Hawkeye's sharpest arrow bounced harmlessly away. One by one, the heroes were defeated.

Then Spider-Man remembered what Iron Man had told him: some of the greatest victories have been won by heroes working as a team. That's what they needed! None of them could defeat Thanos alone. But if they teamed up...

"Everybody!" Spider-Man cried. "We need to work together!"

With Spider-Man leading the assault, the heroes all fell in. Each hero brought their greatest strengths to the fight.

"We need to reverse the portal," Spider-Man realised. "Come on, heroes, let's knock this tough Titan into oblivion!"

When the Super Heroes worked as one, they were an invincible army!

In the fiercest battle Central Park had ever seen, Spider-Man and his heroic friends banished Thanos to a far-off dimension in the multiverse. The world was safe once more.

"Teaching me my own words of wisdom?" Iron Man asked, slinging a metal-clad arm around Spider-Man's shoulders. "You're a pretty smart kid."

"Yeah, maybe even smarter than you." Spider-Man smiled.

"Hey, now, don't get crazy," Iron Man replied.

Spider-Man had finally won his place among the greatest heroes of the age, but it wasn't on his own. Spider-Man teamed up and saved the world!

Mysterio's Revenge

One day, Peter Parker was late for work. As Spider-Man, he was swinging through New York towards the Daily Bugle.

As he neared the building, he saw an explosion of green smoke erupt from the top floor!

His spider-sense instantly tingled as he landed on the building and peered through the broken window.

"Now that I have your attention," the bizarre voice said,
"you will all witness the total destruction of the Daily Bugle!"
Spider-Man recognised that voice – it was his enemy
Mysterio, the master of illusion! The menacing Mysterio
was holding J. Jonah Jameson by the tie and addressing the
terrified staff.

"No one can help you now, Jameson, not even
Spider-Man!" the villain hissed.

"That's my cue!" Spidey said as he launched himself at the villain. Spider-Man caught Mysterio by surprise, and the two tumbled to the ground, locked in combat!

As the Super Hero and Super Villain continued to fight, Jameson crawled to the exit.

He jiggled the doorknob frantically, but all the doors had been locked from the outside.

They were trapped!

"The Amazing Spider-Man!" Mysterio began.
"You're right on time... to meet your doom!"

Mysterio raised his arms and the newsroom
filled with thick, green smoke.

Then the villain disappeared into the fog
right before everyone's eyes!

"Meet my doom?" Spider-Man said.
"What do you suppose he meant by that?"

Mysterio's voice echoed eerily across the room. "Last I saw you, J. Jonah Jameson, you promised that you could deliver Spider-Man," the villain said. "Instead, I was defeated by Spider-Man... and now, you will all pay!"

With that, Mysterio appeared through the smoke and lunged at J. Jonah Jameson.

Spider-Man knew he had to act fast! He fired a web and swung towards the villain. With unbelievable strength and speed, the Amazing Spider-Man kicked Mysterio in the chest and then fired another web at Jameson, sticking him to the wall.

"Sorry to disappoint you, Mysterio, but I don't have plans to meet my doom for at least another sixty or seventy years!" Spidey said.

Spider-Man stood above the trapped Mysterio and removed the villain's glass helmet. But Spidey was shocked at the person he saw beneath the mask: it was Peter Parker!

"Parker!" Jameson yelled. "You're Mysterio?!"

Mysterio was a master of disguise, but only Spider-Man knew that the villain wasn't really Peter Parker. *This must've been the disguise he was going to use in order to escape*, Spidey thought.

But how was Spider-Man going to save everyone in the Daily Bugle and prove that Mysterio wasn't Peter?

While all these thoughts ran through Spidey's mind, the villain leapt forwards and attacked!

Ow, I hit hard! Spidey thought. As he tried to pick himself up off the floor, Mysterio delivered another hard blow. *I can't believe I'm beating myself up!* Spider-Man was dazed, but he rolled across the smoky room.

With Mysterio distracted by his precious helmet, Spidey looked around the office and realised the only person who wasn't there was the real Peter Parker.

That's why Mysterio used him for his disguise! And that gave the wall-crawler an idea.

Spidey jumped across the room and crawled along the wall, completely hidden by the smoke. He grabbed a hoodie off a desk, zipped it up to cover his suit and removed his mask.

Now it looked like the real Peter Parker had shown up. "Hey, guys. Sorry I'm late."

Mysterio turned, enraged. "No! How did you get in?"

"*Two* Parkers?" Jameson said, confused. "Next there will be *two* Spider-Men!"

"Not if I have anything to say about it!" Mysterio said.

The appearance of the real Peter Parker had worked. While everyone was distracted, Peter ducked beneath the smoke, put his mask back on and charged at Mysterio.

Firing both web-shooters again and again, the Amazing Spider-Man captured Mysterio in a giant spiderweb for all to see.

Then, with a CRASH, the police finally broke into the newsroom, just as Spider-Man jumped out the nearest window. "Here you go, boys," Spidey said to the cops as he swung away.

"One gift-wrapped Super Villain, courtesy of you-know-who!"

A few minutes later, the real Peter Parker entered the newsroom. J. Jonah Jameson, who was still stuck to the side of the wall, looked down at him. "Parker," Jameson said, "you're late!" Peter sighed. It was just another day at the office for Peter Parker... and your friendly neighbourhood Spider-Man!

Dark Webs

"WAHOO!" Spider-Man shouted at the top of his lungs.
"What a great afternoon for a swing."

Spidey was on his way to meet Miles Morales and Gwen Stacy for a Super Hero training session.

"Hey, I need help down here!" an old woman shouted from the street.

Time to help the people of New York City,

Spider-Man thought, swooping down from above.

The old woman grabbed him by the arm,

pointing to a sewer grate.

"There's a goo monster down there, Spider-Kid,"

she said. "Get it out."

"The name is actually Spider-Ma'am, uh,

um, I mean Spider-Man," he said. "And that

thing you're smelling? It isn't a goo monster.

That's just our wonderfully stinky city."

After changing out of his suit, Peter Parker joined Gwen and Miles at the Midtown High science lab.

"Hey, pals. What have we got?" he asked cheerfully.

Peter noticed the curious device Gwen was tinkering with. "What's that thing?" he asked.

"Just a sound cannon Miles is helping me work on," Gwen said. "I'm putting the final touches on the battery pack now."

"Awesome! But we better get going," Peter said.

Once they were on the roof, Spider-Man said, "Today, we're going to go through a couple of simple training exercises. Make sure to pay attention. You've got to work hard if you want to be a Super Hero."

Spider-Man got Miles and Gwen, whose Super Hero name was Ghost-Spider, to perform lots of different exercises, like press-ups and skipping.

"Enough exercises," said Miles. "I want to show you guys my bio-electric venom blasts."

Miles tried them out on Spider-Man, but the agile hero jumped and flipped away from them all.

Spider-Man wasn't impressed. "Looks like you guys need more training than I thought."

Suddenly, on the street below, long black tendrils appeared out of the sewers. They began throwing unsuspecting citizens into the air.

"Uh-oh," said Miles. He spun a web that caught the citizens before they hit the ground. "That was close."

"What's happening, Spidey?" asked Ghost-Spider.

The three of them looked down to the streets and saw...

... VENOM!

"That's the alien symbiote that bonded itself to a human host named Eddie Brock!" exclaimed Ghost-Spider.

Spider-Man tried to reason with Eddie, but it was impossible. Venom had complete control of his body.

With no other choice, the three of them jumped down to confront the alien menace before it hurt someone.

The trio began fighting Venom, while also protecting the citizens trying to escape the carnage.

Confidently, Spider-Man shot Venom in the face with his sticky webbing. "My newest batch is stronger than ever," Spidey called out to his friends. As far as he was concerned, their troubles were nearly over and Venom would soon be beaten.

He was wrong.

SWACK!

Venom had ripped off the webbing and thumped Spider-Man with his powerful black tendrils.

The Super Hero had been knocked out cold. Miles and Ghost-Spider pulled Spider-Man to safety. It was up to the two of them to stop Venom now.

"I think I know how to take Venom down for good," Ghost-Spider said to Miles. "But I'll need you to keep him distracted for a couple of minutes."

As Ghost-Spider swung away, Miles noticed a brightly lit sign hanging above the alien. He fired a round of bio-electric blasts at the sign, sending sparks raining down on Venom.

Ghost-Spider was back in the lab where she retrieved her sound cannon. "You and I are going to save the day," Ghost-Spider said excitedly to the cannon.

She checked it one more time, before heading back to where Miles and Venom were fighting.

"Plug your ears," said Ghost-Spider, as she landed between Miles and Venom.

She then unleashed the full power of the sound cannon on the symbiote and it started to lose its monstrous form.

"Make it sssssstop!" screeched Venom.

Soon, Venom's body reverted to a puddle of goo, revealing Eddie Brock's human form underneath.

The police rushed to the scene and took Eddie to jail.

Ghost-Spider was relieved the sound cannon had worked.

Now it was time to check Spider-Man was okay.

"What happened?" asked Spider-Man, groggily. He'd only just woken up after being hit by Venom.

"Ghost-Spider saved the day," explained Miles. "She used her sound cannon to turn Venom back into goo."

"I couldn't have done it without your help," said Ghost-Spider, modestly.

Even in his confused state, Spider-Man felt bad for not believing his friends were ready to help him fight crime.

"A real hero needs to fight smart, like both of you did," said Spider-Man, proudly. "I'm glad we're a team."

Suddenly, the old lady from earlier in the day appeared.

"I told you so, Spider-Man!" she cried. "It was a goo monster all along!"

"Who's that?" asked Miles.

Spidey cringed. "Just one of my fans. Shall we go?"

The three heroes cheered as they swung into the sky, ready to fight crime together.